P9-DGX-229

SEP 2 1 2001

WITHDRAWN
Public Library
Baldwinsville, NY

Warthogs
in the Kitchen

A Sloppy Counting Book

Pamela Duncan Edwards
Illustrated by Henry Cole

Hyperion Books for Children
New York

Text © 1998 by Pamela Duncan Edwards.
Illustrations © 1998 by Henry Cole.

All rights reserved. No part of this book may be reproduced or transmitted in any
form or by any means, electronic or mechanical, including photocopying, recording,
or by any information storage and retrieval system, without written permission from
the publisher. For information address Hyperion Books for Children,
114 Fifth Avenue, New York, New York 10011-5690.

Printed in Hong Kong by South China Printing Company (1988) Limited

SEP 2 1 2001 This book is set in 28-point Bookman.
The artwork for each picture was prepared using pen,
colored pencils, and watercolor paint.

FIRST EDITION
3 5 7 9 10 8 6 4 2

Library of Congress Cataloging-in-Publication Data
Edwards, Pamela Duncan.
Warthogs in the kitchen / Pamela Duncan Edwards ; illustrated by Henry Cole.
p.   cm.
Summary: Three warthogs count to ten as they bake cupcakes.
ISBN 0-7868-0399-1 (trade)—ISBN 0-7868-2351-8 (lib. bdg.)
[1. Warthog—Fiction. 2. Baking—Fiction. 3. Counting. 4. Stories in rhyme.]
I. Cole, Henry, ill. II. Title.
PZ8.3.E283War   1998
[E]—dc21   97-27301

For Calum Ross Pickett,
with all my love.
—P. D. E.

To Rachel,
newest cupcake in the family.
—H. C.

1

One little chef thinks
he'll cook today.

2

Two clean hooves.
All the germs washed away.

"I want to help.
I won't make a mess."

"Better find some measures.
We can't just guess."

3

Three cake makers read the
book to check how.

4

Four scoops of sugar should
go in now.

There's something in the bowl
that shouldn't be there!

"Get out this instant, you greedy little bear."

5

Five scoops of butter.
Beat and beat some more.

6

Six cracked eggs.
How many on the floor?

"I've found a jar of pickles!
Should pickles go in, too?"

"Pickles in cupcakes!
Well, perhaps just a few!"

7

Seven scoops of flour should
make the mixture just right.

8

Eight pink tongues lick lips
at the sight.

"Put them in the cupcake pans.
Let's each have a turn."

"Pop them in the oven.
Don't let them burn!"

9

Nine minutes cooking and
our cakes will be ready.

10

Ten cupcakes—the two tiny
ones for Teddy.

O

Zero cakes left.
They're down in each tummy.

"We're excellent cooks.
Those cupcakes were YUMMY!"

CUPCAKE RECIPE FOR HUMANS

$1/2$ cup butter or margarine

$1/2$ cup sugar

2 eggs

$1/2$ cup self-rising flour

$1/2$ teaspoon baking powder

1. Beat butter and sugar together until light and creamy.
2. Add one egg and beat well.
3. Add the other egg plus a spoonful of flour, and beat.
4. Sift the remaining flour and baking powder together.
5. Mix lightly into the creamed mixture.
6. Put big spoonfuls into ten cupcake pans.
7. Bake in the oven for about 25 minutes at 350 degrees.
8. Turn out onto a cookie sheet to cool.
9. Decorate with some frosting.
10. Serve with lemonade to your very favorite people.

CUPCAKE RECIPE FOR WARTHOGS

4 scoops of sugar—use any scoop you can find—sand shovels are great.
5 scoops of butter—if you don't have butter, use chocolate syrup.
2 eggs—some warthogs like to remove the shells first.
7 scoops of flour—see who can get the most flour on their nose.
Add anything else you can find in the pantry: pickles, peanut butter, mustard. Brussels sprouts taste especially nice.

1. Wash hooves.
2. Tell your friends they can help.
3. Put sugar in bowl, add butter. Go play tag with your friends.
4. Remove any stray teddy bear you find in the bowl.
5. Throw eggs into bowl—throw as many as you want, but the warthog that gets two in the bowl first is the winner.
6. Add the flower—buttercups, dandelions—wait a minute—we mean "flour," of course!
7. Put the mixture into cupcake pans—Warthog Little League pitchers are very good at this.
8. Lick bowl. Lick measuring spoons. Lick countertop. Lick recipe book. Lick your friends.
9. Cook cakes until you can't wait any longer.
10. Eat cakes quickly before they're stolen by a teddy bear.